THE DREAM CHAMPION

LESLEY FISHER

Author's Tranquility Press
ATLANTA, GEORGIA

Copyright © 2024 by Lesley Fisher

All rights reserved. No part of this publication may be reproduced, distributed or transmitted in any form or by any means, including photocopying, recording, or other electronic or mechanical methods, without the prior written permission of the publisher, except in the case of brief quotations embodied in critical reviews and certain other noncommercial uses permitted by copyright law. For permission requests, write to the publisher, addressed "Attention: Permissions Coordinator," at the address below.

Lesley Fisher/Author's Tranquility Press
3900 N Commerce Dr. Suite 300 #1255
Atlanta, GA 30344
www.authorstranquilitypress.com

Ordering Information:
Quantity sales. Special discounts are available on quantity purchases by corporations, associations, and others. For details, contact the "Special Sales Department" at the address above.

The Dream Champion/Lesley Fisher
Paperback: 978-1-964362-89-2
eBook: 978-1-964037-67-7

CONTENTS

CHAPTER 1 Max "G" 1
CHAPTER 2 Friends 5
CHAPTER 3 Wild Imagination 8
CHAPTER 4 Heavy Breathing 12
CHAPTER 5 "Phobetor" and "Morpheus" 16
CHAPTER 6 Run Away 20
CHAPTER 7 Hiding 24
CHAPTER 8 Thoughts 27
CHAPTER 9 Home 30
CHAPTER 10 The Bribe 33
CHAPTER 11 The Aunts 37
CHAPTER 12 The Garden 40
CHAPTER 13 Tilly 44
CHAPTER 14 "Oh No!" 49
CHAPTER 15 "The Fight" 53
CHAPTER 16 Angel 58
CHAPTER 17 Nellie 62
CHAPTER 18 Dragon Down 65
CHAPTER 19 Other Champions 69

The dream....

It was very dark, but they all started that way! It took some time, but he knew that it would show itself soon enough! There in the dark he could hear a vicious roar! The roar was so loud he could feel it tremble all through him! Here it comes, he thinks to himself. "Come on! Show yourself, I know you are here!" He yells out to whatever is about to show itself! Soon there is a glimpse! Then there is fire! It is all around him! He can almost feel the heat from it! The boy looks around to see if he can get a glimpse of it, but it is hiding in the shadows. "Where are you!" he yells. "Are you afraid of a little boy?" he asks the entity that he knows is there. This provokes the nightmarish creature to show itself!

Now, most boys who dream of such creatures would wake up trembling from the sight, but not this boy! This boy was used to these creatures, he fought them every night. He knew he would have the skills and weapons to fight whatever it was that showed up in his dream! He learned a long time ago that they could not hurt him if he was brave enough to stand and fight! He also learned that all he had to do was think of whatever he needed, and it would materialize out of nowhere to help him fight!

Finally, he could see what it was! It was a smoke dragon with blazing yellow eyes! Lizard eyes! It flew all around him roaring its vicious roar and blowing fire! The boy only had to think for a moment! "What do I need to fight this creature?" Then it comes to him! He will need fire resistant armor and a magic sword that will kill a magic smoke beast! Both of these things materialize for him, and he is now ready to fight the creature circling him!

Only one problem! The beast is way up in the air flying around and he is on the ground, how can he get up there? He wonders. Of course, he could just think to himself that he could fly, but he was more creative than that! He imagined a great big, huge swing that was swinging as high as the dragon! When it came down to his level, he jumped on the swing which gave him enough momentum to fly at the smoke dragon and stab it in the chest with one clean jab! Thus, the smoke dragon vanished with one last roar! The boy landed on his feet as he always did and held up his sword and yelled "Victory!"

He then woke......

CHAPTER 1
Max "G"

Do you remember a time when you felt really amazing? A time when you did something you thought could make you burst with pride! I'm talking about the times when you go out of your way to help another, not for gain of something, but because it just felt like the right thing to do. Maybe you saved a friend from a bully at school or helped an elderly person when they needed someone to help. Who knows what it was, but at the time it made you feel like a champion, a hero of sorts! You thought it was the most wonderful feeling ever!

Let me introduce you to, Max "G"! Max "G" is a boy of 11 years, and he is our champion of this story. You are probably wondering what the "G" stands for? Well, let me tell you Max's story.

Max is an orphan who was adopted by a couple named Garry and Nancy Anderson. Max was so happy the day they came and got him from the orphanage. He has lived with the Andersons for 2 years now. They are good people. They treat Max like he is their very own son, and they love him, as he loves them in return.

It was only a few weeks after the day he was adopted by the Anderson's that Max was struck down by a speeding car on his way to school. The car was going so fast that the driver lost control and veered onto the sidewalk, the sidewalk that Max was walking on and smashed right into him!

Max almost died that day, but someone, somewhere – a guardian angel maybe, knew he was special and helped him get better. He had quite the head injury, but after some time he fully recovered. The doctors told Max's new parents that it was because of the injuries that Max endured, that he was always having the nightmarish dreams! That the dreams would eventually fade and would not be so pronounced. Max had only to realize the dreams would and could not hurt him in any way! To be brave and they would eventually stop.

Max learned to deal with the dreams in his own special way and is now used to having them. They don't seem to bother him anymore! But that is not what we were talking about. We were talking about the "G" in Max "G".

One day when Max was bored, and his mother and father had left to go to the neighbors for coffee, Max decided to do some exploring around the house.

For some reason Max was always told to never go into his dad's study unless his mom or dad was there, and he was asked to enter. It's not like he had never been in his dad's study before, but he always wondered why his parents didn't like him to go in there. He always felt as if his new parents were hiding something from him.

So, Max did the one thing he shouldn't have and went into his dad's study and had a good look around. He didn't find anything too amazing or anything too special, not until he opened a drawer in his father's desk and found an old, beat-up piece of paper that was yellowed and blackened around the edges, it had looked as if it had been in a fire. There was quite a bit of information missing, all Max could read was that it was a marriage certificate for someone, the names were Paul and Angela "G".

In his heart he felt that this piece of paper meant something to him. He knew deep down that this was his real parents. It was at this time that his adoptive parents decided to come home and caught him looking at the piece of paper. Neither one seemed mad but were shocked.

"Max, I thought I told you to never come in here!" his father said in a very slow, low voice.

Max knew then that he had found what it was his parents were hiding from him. He grasped the paper to his chest and ran passed his parents and out of the study! He went straight to his room where he just stared at the piece of paper for hours. At first, he cried, but then he said to himself out loud, "why are you crying, silly really, you knew you were adopted." Then he reasoned, "Yes, but you never thought about your real parents before, you were always told no one knew anything about them. Everyone lied to you!"

This angered Max, but he was also extremely happy at the same time. His parents were real! And this made all the difference.

Max just sat on his bed and wondered about the two people on the paper. Paul and Angela "G". He spent many hours just pondering what the "G" stood for, that he kept saying it over and over again. "G, G. I bet it's something wonderful and mysterious," he would say out loud to himself. "Something like Graham, or Green like the Green Hornet!" Then in his mind he would say, unlike Garry and Nancy Anderson, their names were just so ordinary and regular. After a while Max decided he liked not knowing what the "G" stood for, he liked that he could be anybody.

When his adopted parents came to Max later to talk about the paper, they told him that when they went to adopt him, the nuns that ran the orphanage gave them the piece of paper and told them that was all they had left of the fire that killed his parents, that no one really knew who they were or what their last names were. When no one came forward to look after the enfant baby that was rescued from the fire, they guessed that Max was all that was left of their family. His new parents went on to tell Max that they were eventually going to show him the paper but were going to wait until he was a little older, for they didn't think he was ready, especially after his accident, but that they were going to give it to him when he turned 18, and he could do whatever he wanted with it. It was his to decide.

So, he kept the paper and put it in a special place where no one else would find it! Thus, he began calling himself Max "G".

CHAPTER 2
Friends

When Max G first moved to the little town of Minnedosa, it took him a long time to meet any friends, for people did not know how to treat him, he was the adopted little boy who had been hit by a car, and now had crazy dreams. But eventually all the people in Minnedosa warmed up to Max G and thought he was quite alright. Of course, there are always going to be those people who can't deal with those who are different. Max G didn't mind though, he stayed away from them, and they stayed away from him. It was a mutual relationship!

Max G in spite of it all managed to get a couple of good friends, Jamie and Lukas. Jamie was a tough little guy with short brown hair and always wore a baseball cap. His pants and hat always seem to match. If he wore green pants than his hat was green. He was always threatening to "give that guy a fat lip" whoever it was that made him mad that day. Jamie always seemed to want fight, even though he never got into a fight. Max G didn't think Jamie would know what to do if someone actually tried to fight him.

Lukas was the total opposite; he was skinny boy with blond hair that fell over his eyes. His clothes never matched, and they always seemed to be two sizes too big for him. Probably because he had two older brothers and he had to wear hand me downs. Lukas never wanted to fight, and he liked reading and playing on his computer. Oh, and he lived next door to Max G.

One particular Saturday afternoon the three boys had decided they were going to go down to the river and do some fishing. They were sitting waiting for the fish to bite when Lukas called them over yelling, "come and have a look at this!" Sitting on Lukas's lap was his laptop, he never went anywhere without it. Even fishing.

When Max G and Jamie moved over to where Lukas was, they looked at the caption on his laptop. On the screen of his laptop was a news cast from California, a place that was a whole state away from where the three boys were now. It was talking about how another bad guy vanished in thin air. The lady was saying, "It seems a family had been in the midst of being burglarized by a bad man named Jon Sommer. A bad man that the police had been looking for, for some time. He had tied up a family in their living room, so he could ransack the place without any interruption, when out of nowhere he just vanishes right in front of the family, leaving all the things he collected through the house there. At first the family thought it was a trick of some kind and was afraid to try and move, but after some time they knew it wasn't a trick and had managed to get out of their bonds and call police. Even the police did not know what to make of it, for even with extensive searches they have not been able to find the vanished criminal."

"What do you think of that?" asks Lukas.

"So what!" says Jamie? "It doesn't involve us, it's way over in California, who cares!"

Lukas looks over at Jamie like he has a hole in his head. "A guy just vanishes out of thin air, and you don't think that is amazing! I have been watching the news every day, and every day it seems another bad guy just vanishes. And it's not just in California. It has been all over the world! China, Hawaii, Vancouver, Ontario! And many other places! The top guys, you know government officials, and such are making a big deal out of it. No one knows what is happening to these people! It is making people frightened! What if next time it isn't a bad guy and whatever it is starts to take ordinary people!"

At this Jamie looks a little more frightened, but shakes it off, for he is the tough guy. "So, what! It will probably never happen here anyways!" he says and turns and goes back over to his fishing rod to see if anything is on it.

Max G looks over at Lukas and says, "Don't mind him, he probably is frightened but doesn't want to show it, is all! Sure makes you wonder what could be happening, though!"

"What if it's aliens?" asks Lukas, with a look of excitement on his face!

At this comment Jamie looks over and says "That would be so cool! Do you think that is what it is?"

Lukas responds back with, "Well the officials are definitely looking into everything! They are not ruling anything out!"

But it is at this time that Lukas's rod starts to move. "Hey Lukas, I think you caught something!" yells Jamie from his spot on the bank. Lukas gets up and passes his laptop over to Max G and runs for his rod. As Lukas fights with his rod Max G keeps looking at the news casting. He looks at the time the man disappears, and wonders about it. He feels in his guts that this has something to do with him but can't figure out how it could possibly be.

He closes the article and the laptop and goes over to where Lukas has finally pulled the fish in. It is only a small bottom feeder but the look on Lukas's face was of pure happiness, you would have thought he caught a whale. You see this was Lukas's first fish. It really wasn't big enough to eat, but Lukas wanted to take it home to show his brothers and dad anyway. Both Jamie and Max G pat Lukas on the back and say, "Way to go!"

CHAPTER 3
Wild Imagination

That evening at supper Max G is sitting with his family and they are discussing current events. This usually meant talking about what was going on in Minnedosa that day. Which meant that Max G would tell his parents about Lukas's fish that he caught, and his parents would talk about the garden or what the neighbors did that day. Things like that!

It was when Max G brought up the news cast that both parents went quiet. Then they shook it off and Max G's father said "Max you are way too young to be worrying about things like that! You should not have read that clipping. It is not for young boys with wild imaginations to be reading up on!"

Then his mother chimes in with, "There is a reason why your father and I don't let you watch the news or read the newspapers, there is too many scary things going on in the world today, and you have enough terror in your life now with all those nightmares that you have every night!"

Max takes a deep frustrated breath, rolls his eyes then responds back, "Mom, I am fine, the dreams are not that scary anymore! Really! I have been able to get through them without feeling so scared anymore! I am actually feeling okay!"

"It does not matter that you are able to handle them, you are still having them. And until they are completely gone you will do as we say. We know what is best for you. Please Max don't watch or read these things. They are only going to cause your dreams to get worse!" Pleads his father. But continues with, "Do you not remember what the doctor said, he told us to make sure you stayed away from scary movies, or books that we thought might cause the dreams to get worse. This we have done! Now you must try and do the same. Please Max G forget what you have read and play a much happier game with your friends for now. There will be time enough for you to learn the lessons of the world!"

Max G knew his father was serious for he even said, "Max G". He usually only calls him "Max," for he does not like the fact that Max has taken on the "G". He deems it silly! Especially when Max has a last name now. His father told him that he thought the last name they gave him was a good last name and the "Max" should not be ashamed of it. His adoptive father would never understand that Max wasn't ashamed of his new name, but that he felt a closeness to his real parents when used the "G" in his name. It was just one of those things. He told his father that he liked the name "Anderson", but he felt he also needed to use the "G" as well.

At this Max G's mother decided to interrupt and change the subject to a better one. "Who wants dessert? Strawberry Shortcake!" As she gets up to clear the supper plates and bring in the dessert. Both boy and man stop their intense talk and yell "I do!" as if they are little children. Both knew that this meant subject closed. Mom had had enough. They went on to talk about happier things.

That evening Max G went to his bedroom to play some video games while waiting for his mom and dad to wash the supper dishes. It being Saturday evening meant family night. They were either going to rent a movie, go to a movie, or stay home and play some kind of game. Sometimes it was video games, sometimes board games or just plain old card games. Whatever they picked last week from the choice jar.

The choice jar was full of activities, and every Saturday after they were done with their family night, they would pick another activity in which they would do the next week. No matter what, that was the activity they would do, no backing out! Which was the reason for the week in advance notice.

While Max G was sitting playing his PlayStation Three - a racing game of some kind, something started scratching furiously at his window. This startles Max, so he put his game on pause and gets up to have a look. When he pulled the curtain aside, he almost jumped across the room. Right outside his window were great big, bright yellow eyes – lizard eyes! Max quickly closes the curtain and jumps back, then starts to scream for his dad, who immediately came running right up!

"What! What is it!" his father says out of breath, for he ran the stairs as fast as he could. Max G just points to his window. So his dad went over and pulled the curtain open and could see – nothing! There was nothing there! "I don't see anything!" he told Max G.

Max G came over and had a look. His dad was right, there was nothing there. But he was sure it was there. His dad turned and smiled at Max G and patted him on the shoulder and said, "Must have been your imagination son!"

"Yeah, must have been!" he says back, not really convinced.

"Your mother and I are almost done. Why don't you come down and set up the board? You know it takes a little while to set up the bank and what not for Monopoly," his dad says with a little nervous chuckle. Trying to make it out like it was nothing and that it was okay to be a little startled.

"Yeah okay, I'm just going to turn off my game and will be right down!" says Max G.

"Good then, see you in a few!" Says his father as he leaves the room.

Max G is still a little shaken, he was sure that the creature was there. But then how can that be, they only come to him in his dreams. His dad was right it was only his imagination! Even so, Max G went and had another look out the window just to be sure, and sure enough there was nothing. "Whew!" he said to himself and went down to play Monopoly with his family.

CHAPTER 4
Heavy Breathing

Mr. Anderson seemed to have a knack for the game of Monopoly, as he was kicking butt and was beating Mrs. Anderson and Max G rather badly. He pretty much owned everything and had all the money. Max and his mom were just about to say "enough," when something happened that scared the life out of Max G.

Something very large seemed to be standing right behind him, Max G could hear its low growling! It wasn't a very loud growl, but its rumble was so harsh Max could feel it all through his body! It was enough that even his parents should have heard it or at least felt it. He asked them, "Can you hear that?"

Max G's mom looked at him with a smile on her face, for she had just finished giving her husband the once over in a very jokingly manor, she then turns and asks Max with a smile on her face "hear what hon?"

Max G couldn't believe they couldn't hear it, it seemed to be getting closer. He looked over at his father, "that growling, can't you hear it?"

Max G's father looked at him like he was playing a joke on him! "Now Max, the joke is over, you know there is no growling, and there was nothing outside as well. You will give yourself worse nightmares if you keep talking like that. You should have never read that news clipping!"

Then as if to close the matter at hand his father asks them, "Now does everyone forfeit or should we continue?" Then he rubs his hands together and smirks at them, as if to say, "or are you gluttons for more punishment!"

Max G can't concentrate on the game anymore or his parents, as the growling seems to have gotten louder and much closer. It is getting harder to hear what they are saying, not only that; with the growling is coming great big, long breaths. Breaths that are actually making everything around them move! Max G can feel it on the back of his neck and back. They are getting so much bigger by the moment that it is also moving his parent's hair, and fluttering their clothes, as well as sending everything on the table flying!

Max G is now so terrified that he can't move! His parents are talking to him as if nothing is happening and this scares him, for how could they not notice? Max was asking himself, what the heck is happening? He knows there is some kind of creature breathing its heavy breath right behind him, but he is too frightened to even get up and have a look.

Then when the breathing and growling become extremely unbearable, his parents just stop talking. They look at Max G as if trying to figure out what is wrong with him, for they can see the terrified expression on his face. But then they both get blank looks on their faces and lie their heads on the table and fall fast asleep.

Max G tries to call to them, "Mom, dad, are you okay?" But of course, neither one answers. Max G is alone with whatever has decided to haunt him, and it takes every bit of strength he can muster to jump up and run. Not once looking behind him, he just runs up the stairs to the first bedroom he can get to. His parent's room!

Once inside he slams the door shut and dives under their bed. He hasn't been this frightened in a long, long time. He doesn't understand what is going on! Why are his nightmare creatures coming to his awakened world? How can they just show up at his house and put his parents to sleep? Does this mean he is sleeping, and is this just another nightmare? Is he going to have to fight them like in his dreams? He's just so frightened he can't think properly.

"Okay!" he says to himself, "think; think what to do!"

As he is lying under the bed he is trying to get his head straight. "Calm down! You must think what to do! First, I am just going to sit here for a few minutes and catch my breath. Then I am...." He stops talking out loud to himself because at that moment he hears something just outside the door of his parent's room! Something is scratching, and sniffing, with a kind of snuffling.

Oh no! It's real! He thinks to himself. For some reason he was still under the impression that this couldn't be happening, and his parents were downstairs doing their normal things. But from the sounds of things, he was wrong. He is now so stressed he starts to cry; he just does not know what to do!

Then out of nowhere he hears two voices bickering, at first, he thinks it is his parents and everything is going to be alright, but then as he listens a little closer, he realizes there is no way these voices can belong to his parents. They sound very manly and have a hollowness to them. Try to imagine if you could talk to a god, what a god's voice would be like. Booming and loud, right? Well, that is sort of what these voices were getting to be as they got louder by the minute.

At first Max G thought they were downstairs, then outside, but now it sounded as if they were in the room with him. "He can't play your game; he is just a boy!" one of the voices was saying.

"It is only because you won't give him a chance, I am giving him the chance he needs! How else can he become our champion?" Argues the other voice.

Champion? What the heck were these voices talking about? Max G wonders, and continues to listen, but for some reason things have gone silent. Then there is a bright light that shines through the whole room and one of the voices says, "Come out champion, you must not hide!"

Max G stopped crying when he first heard the two voices, but now he has started to shake. Everything is shaking and he can't stop. Did that voice really just ask him to come out? Did it really call him a champion? He wasn't a champion that he knew of?

"I will not ask again, come out or there will be serious consequences!" says the voice sounding a little bored and perturbed at the same time!

Max G decides he had better come out and see what is going on, even though he was shaking uncontrollably and couldn't stop. He crawls out from under his parent's bed and can't believe what he sees! There standing in front of him is a glowing man, and in the mirror is another glowing man, both looking very serious, and Max G finds himself even more scared!

CHAPTER 5
"Phobetor" and "Morpheus"

"Well boy, do you think you are up to the challenge?" says the glowing man standing in front of him.

"SSSir! WWWWhat cccchallenge!" stutters Max G, shaking like a leaf.

"Come! Don't play games with me! Are you to be our next champion or not!" replies the glowing man.

It is at this time the glowing man in the mirror decides to butt in. "Icelus, can't you see the boy is already terrified and he doesn't even know what you want of him?"

"How could he not, Morpheus; we have been challenging him all this time." The glowing man that the other called Icelus argues back!

"Look at him, he is in the dark. He does not know that you created all those creatures in his dreams, let alone why they were there. It is obvious he doesn't even know who we are!" Then he looks over at Max G and says, "do you boy?" asks the other glowing man, the one in the mirror, the one the other glowing man called Morpheus.

"No sir, I don't!" says Max G, who at that moment felt he deserved to know, so stands up straight and stops shaking, then asks "who are you?"

"Really," says the glowing man outside the mirror. But he looks at the other glowing man in the mirror for a second and gets a nod from him. "Oh alright, I can't believe he doesn't know who we are. I thought all humans knew who we are!"

The other glowing man in the mirror admonishes the other glowing man, "Phobetor!"

"Alright, my name is Phobetor, but my brothers call me Icelus, I am the God of Nightmares!" At this he says very loudly and turns himself into a beast with a long straight tail, with barbs on the end. The beast has pointy ears and fur all over. It also has donkey hooves for feet and eagle claws for hands. The color of its fur is red, and it has yellow dragon eyes!

It was one of the scariest things that Max G had ever seen, but it did not scare him as much as he thought it should. Mostly it was the complete change from glowing man to this beast that startled him. When it happened Max G just said "Whoa! That's a pretty neat trick, I wish I could do that!"

"See, the boy didn't even frighten!" Says Phobetor.

"Icelus, you are not done telling him who we are!" says the glowing man in the mirror getting very irritated with Phobetor.

"Yes, yes! I am getting there, I just wanted to see how the boy would react is all," completely ignoring the man in the mirror.

"Anyway!" says Phobetor as he turns himself back into a glowing man. "I am the God of Nightmares, Phobetor; and this..," as he points to the mirror, "is my brother, Morpheus; he is the God of Dreams! We are from the land of death; we reside in the place where people go when they die. It is their dream state, or death state! All people go here, but not all people are challenged to become champions. Most just wonder the lands. Some find what they are looking for, and some don't! But either way when you die that is where you go, no matter what! Do you understand now?"

"You want me to become a champion of the underworld, where people go to die? Is that what you are asking me to do?" asks Max G?

"Now he's got it!" says Phobetor.

"I still don't understand, what does a champion do in the underworld?" asks Max G.

At this, Phobetor rolls his eyes and says "come on boy! What do champions usually do?"

"Champions are people who win things, things like races and things like that." Max G. answers.

"Yes, but there is other kinds champions as well. Like the ones who do things unselfishly for other people, the ones who become heroes, those are the ones that win at all costs, no matter what gets in their way." Explains Phobetor. "That is what I want to train you for, to win at all costs!" exclaims Phobetor.

"Win what! What am I winning against?" asks Max G.

At this Morpheus jumps into the conversation and explains. "What my brother wants is for you to help fight the monsters that are trying to take over the underworld. He seems to think that you have a great ability to fight the nightmare creatures that people conjure up! As God of nightmares, Phobetor must bring them to life, whether he wants to or not! So he is always on the lookout for his next champion to help rid the underworld of the vile things! But as I have explained to my brother, you are too young for such a responsibility, and I don't think you are ready for such a task!"

"I am with Morpheus, he is right, I am not ready!" stammers Max G a little frightened. Well maybe a lot frightened!

"Come now," says Phobetor, you have beaten every nightmare creature that I have sent to you in your dreams. There is no reason why you can't beat them here!"

"Here! Like in the awakened world, you want me to fight them here! Are you nuts! I will die!" screams Max G. "I am not ready to die!"

"That is what I was telling my brother, but he doesn't listen. Without our help you couldn't possibly win against such monsters, but he thinks you need real live training! So what does Phobetor do, he gives you the power to make bad guys disappear from your world every time you defeat a monster in your dreams, and now these bad guys are turned into the monsters you have been defeating and Phobetor wants you to defeat them here on your awakened plain! I have told him it is not possible! Not without my help, and I can't help if you are not in the dream world!" Says Morpheus shaking his head!

"Well, I believe he can do it! So let us have a test shall we? You have all night to find a way to defeat the shadow dragon. By morning the dragon will disappear. But if you don't defeat him, he will continue to come back at night to fight you, until you have found the way to defeat him! Good luck!'

With that the two glowing men were back in the mirror. The two of them sat and argued for a minute then were gone!

Max G just stood there, wondering what just happened. "Please tell me this was all a nightmare, and I am not just about to fight a fire breathing shadow dragon!" He says to himself.

He looks around, nothing! Then he hears scratching at the door, then out of nowhere the door flies across the room with a line of fire trailing after it!

Max G jumps right out if his skin. Good thing he wasn't standing in front the door, he thinks to himself. But then he looks to where the door was and sees his nightmare come true. The shadow dragon has come, it has come to kill him!

CHAPTER 6
Run Away

Max G couldn't move, it was like his will wasn't his own anymore! In his mind he kept telling his legs to move, he was even screaming at them to move but they just wouldn't respond! He was frozen with fear!

How is he going to fight a shadow dragon like this? He looked over at the shadow dragon and it hadn't come any closer. It seemed to be waiting for him to make the first move! Well, if that was the case Max G was never going to move, ever!

Somehow, this thought helped Max G to relax a little and think. He stopped staring at the doorway and looked around, of course, this little action made the shadow dragon growl. Only growl though, the monstrous thing hadn't moved as of yet.

Good! Thought Max G, maybe I have time to figure out what to do. Obviously, the shadow dragon was giving him this time, which meant that the shadow dragon was confident he was going to get Max G easily! He was playing with his prey, trying to give Max the hope that maybe there was a chance of escape! Either way Max G was going to use the time to his advantage!

Again, he looks around the room, there is absolutely nothing he can use as a weapon. There was the bed, the drawers with the mirror that the two glowing men went into, the closet which was way on the other side of the room and then there was the window. Out of all the choices it looked as if hiding would be somewhat of an option, only the shadow dragon was waiting to see what he was going to do, so really it was no option at all.

The only thing he could think of, was to get to the window, jump out, roll off the roof, then run! Run until he found something to fight the dragon with! What would kill a smoke dragon in the real world? Max G didn't know, so his only option at this point was to run!

He looked over at the dragon, who in turn gave another scary growl, you know, the ones that make the hair on the back of your neck stand up! Max G didn't want the smoke dragon to know what he was thinking. So he spent some time looking at the closet, then the bed, and with each movement, the dragon would give another scary growl. Meanwhile, Max G was weighing how long it would take him to get to the window, unlatch it, roll to the edge of the roof overhang, jump down to the ground. Then run!

Only one problem, once on the ground, which way should he go? This was important, it could definitely be the turning point as to life or death. Max G chose life. Again, he thinks about his plan, once on the ground where should he go? The smoke dragon is huge, but he is a smoke dragon, which means he can practically go anywhere he wants to. So Max G's only option is to find somewhere quick that he doesn't think the smoke dragon will be able to follow. He needs to be able to search for a weapon, and he can't do that with a smoke dragon chasing him the whole time!

So Max racks his brains some more. Where would a smoke dragon not like to go? Then out of nowhere a thought comes to him, and he has an idea that he hopes will work. He suddenly remembers what his town was known for, and this one thing is going to help Max G to escape a fire breathing, smoke dragon.

The thing about the town of Minnedosa, is that it has a beautiful river that runs right through it, which means there are many culverts, these culverts all lead to that river. Well, a smoke dragon would probably not follow someone if they were in water. Right now, in spring the water is running very quickly and fast, this might be Max G's only chance at escape, even though it is probably just as dangerous as trying to fight a smoke dragon! Max G didn't like the thought of all that cold water, and the fight for his life while riding the water to a certain bridge he is hoping to hide under from the dragon. But it was the only thing he could think of.

He can't believe the smoke dragon hasn't tried to attack, but he is grateful. He is also grateful that his new parents Nancy and Garry made sure he had swimming lessons. If they knew what he was about to do, he was sure they would each have a heart attack. They always told him to stay away from the river, it was extremely dangerous. Max G knew this and was totally frightened for his life, but what else was there! It was definitely going to be a long night!

He looked at the smoke dragon once more, then he looked down at his own feet and shuffled from one foot to another a few times, then like a shot he ran to the window which was only two feet from where he was standing. Unlatched the handle and rolled out onto the roof, where he continued to roll to the edge and fall to the ground!

The whole time not looking back. He knew the dragon was surprised by his take off, but he also knew once recovered from his surprise it would charge after him. Sure enough, Max G knows the dragon is upon him. It was now so close to him that when he rolled out on the roof, he could feel the dragon's breath, or maybe it was the wind from his wings. Either way Max G didn't stop, he just kept on rolling.

Once on the ground there was no time to think of the pain that was shooting through the arm he landed on. He needed to get up and run to the culvert and jump in the water. He ran like there was no tomorrow. The whole time knowing the smoke dragon was just above him. It was probably getting ready to blow fire at him or pick him off the ground with his great big claws. Max G didn't stop, and he didn't look back, he just ran!

Finally, he reached the culvert that was just at the end of his street, and he thanked the gods, whatever gods that were listening, that the end of his street was just at the end of his yard. Then without thinking he jumped in and went under the ice-cold water. Man, it was cold! He could feel himself being carried away by the water, when he came up for a breath, he couldn't see the smoke dragon anywhere, but that was because his eyes hadn't adjusted after being in the ice-cold water. Not only that he needed to concentrate so hard on not drowning, but he still tried to look and see where the smoke dragon could have gone!

Finally, he spotted it, the dragon had flown way up in the air, just above where Max G went into the water. Maybe it was trying to see where Max G went, who knows, but it definitely was not following as of yet!

Max G felt some relief, and concentrated on swimming through wild water that was carrying him to the river. By the time he finally got to the river he would be very tired, he didn't think he was going to be able to fight the river. It was much more dangerous than smooth culverts, there was so much debris and rocks, but he was hoping he would be able to snag a branch and bring himself to shore. At least that was what he was hoping for!

He stopped battling with the water and let it take him, he needed to conserve his strength, or he wouldn't have the strength to pull himself out. By the time he got to the river, he was so tired, but he managed to find a branch that took his weight and he pulled himself out. He laid on the ground just under some brush for some time before he even tried to move. He needed to catch his breath. It wasn't until he heard a monstrous cry and growl coming from the skies did he sits up and think about moving! All the time thinking! Oh Man! I am never going to make it! This thing is relentless!

CHAPTER 7
Hiding

Max G watched, terrified; from under the brush, he had been lying under. Watched as the smoke dragon flew in circles looking for its prey. Thank goodness, Max thought, the dragon didn't seem to know where he was. Max thought this was a good sign, he would find somewhere he didn't think the smoke dragon would find him. He looked around and saw a bridge that ran across the river just 100 feet away. He was sure he could make it if he stayed under the brush all the way there.

Max stood and watched the dragon for a few minutes, he wanted to make sure the dragon was looking in the other direction before he even tried to make a dash for the next piece of cover. Max G thought it would have been nice if there was enough brush to be under cover all the way, but it didn't look like that was going to be an option. The brush was only in spots, and even then, it looked as if it would hardly cover him, it was so sparse. The trouble was he wanted to stay as close to the river as possible, as it seemed to be his only escape.

Max G watched as the dragon circled, and finally turned the other way. Then he turned and made a dash for the next piece of brush and dove under it. He laid there waiting, heart hammering so hard he could feel it in his throat. He turned so he was looking up into the sky, he wanted to see if the smoke dragon had seen him. Nope! Max took a deep breath, there it was circling, still trying to find him. Whew! Max felt so relieved to the point he wanted to giggle. But he had to control this urge he knew, for any little noise could make the dragon turn his way, and he just didn't want that!

So Max G kept doing this all the way to the bridge, watch, wait, then dash, look to see if the dragon had seen him. Over and over until he reached a spot that didn't have the best cover, in fact it hardly covered him at all! So when he turned to look to see if the dragon saw him he panicked, for the smoke dragon wasn't circling any more. In fact, it had disappeared! Max G couldn't see it anywhere!

This made Max G scared out of his wits. Where could the monster have gone, why couldn't he see it? He knew that the smoke dragon liked to play with its prey, but he also knew it could be sneaking up on him right now and he would not see it! He got up and started looking around. Nowhere, it was nowhere to be seen. He looked over at the bridge, He was almost there. He asked himself, should he make a run for it?

Max G decided he would definitely make a run for it. At least then he would know if the smoke dragon had spotted him. Knowing for sure that it would lunge or swoop if he saw Max move. So Max G took one last look at the skies and ran! Ran like his life depended on it!

When he finally reached the bridge, he couldn't believe it. The smoke dragon had not chased him or swooped at him. There was nothing, and yet Max G could not hear the dragon or see him anywhere.

Max G did not like the fact he didn't know where the smoke dragon was, for he didn't know if it was sneaking up on him, and about to kill him or not! Anything at this point was possible.

Max G found he couldn't relax enough to think. All he could think about was the stupid smoke dragon coming out of nowhere and eating him or squashing him.

After about an hour, Max decided he would try and stop worrying. He would just try and sit and think of a way to kill the darn thing. But Max G found this to be just too much to think about. His brain had just stopped working, he couldn't think clearly. Not just about how to kill the smoke dragon, but about anything. He was still just too frightened. He had to find a way to calm himself down.

Max sat contemplating on what he should do next. His first thought was to calm down so he could think a little more clearly. So he tried thinking of some of the ways that could help a person to relax. He thought, well; there was counting. He could count to a hundred maybe that would help? So, he started counting, not out loud but in a whisper, just enough so he could hear himself. Which was still pretty hard to do with the river rushing past. He also decided that he wouldn't close his eyes either, for that just made him see too many things that could happen. Such as being taken unawares by a fire breathing dragon!

Once Max G counted to one hundred, he found that "yes" he was much calmer and comes to a conclusion. He just counted to one hundred and there was no sign of the smoke dragon. This must mean that the smoke dragon was nowhere near. That it probably was just somewhere else looking for him. This thought made him feel much better. He started to relax a little and started to think about the events that had transpired. Maybe if he thought things out, something would come to him. Something that would help him to fight a fire breathing, smoke dragon? "Yeah right! Good luck Max G!" he says to himself. "Like that is ever going to happen!"

CHAPTER 8
Thoughts

Max G sat under the bridge it seemed for hours, and it didn't matter how much thought he put to fighting a real smoke dragon, he just could not rap his brain or trick it into thinking he could do so.

There must be a way, the two glowing gods said there was a way. He just had to find it. In his dreams all he had to do was think of what he needed, and it materialized, but that wouldn't happen here? Would it?

Max G thought about it, he would need some fire breathing armor, and a sword that he could use to stab the dragon in the heart. So he closed his eyes and thought really hard about these items. He pictured them clearly in his mind's eye. Hoping beyond hope that when he opened his eyes the items would be there in front of him.

Sure enough, when he opened his eyes there was *nothing*, nothing! Well that settled that! There was no possible way he could fight the darn thing. Guess he was just going to have to run from it forever.

Or was there a way to make fire resistant armor here in the real world, and make some kind of sword out of something here? Where would he find something like that? He thought to himself.

As he was sitting there thinking about things, something very bright started to shine in his eyes. He looked up and sure enough the sun was coming up. But what was shining so bright in his eyes was the glare from a puddle that was just over to his left. The sun was glinting very brightly through the puddle hitting him square in the face.

The glare made Max G get up and decide to try and go home, if the sun was up that must mean the dragon would be gone for the night, right? At least, he hoped this was true as he tried peering out from under the bridge. But even as he peered out from under the bridge it seemed that that puddle glare kept hitting him in the face no matter where he tried to look out. "Sheesh, is that bright!" he says out loud to himself.

"Oh well, no sign of the dragon, guess I will try to go home." Again, he says this out loud to himself, as he has no one else to talk to at this time.

He realizes then, that twice now he has spoken out loud and know dragon attacked. This must mean that it is safe to leave his hiding place.

As he starts his trek home, he realizes that the town is starting to wake up. People are driving down Main Street, and some are walking around or jogging. And what they see is a boy who looks like he has been through a hurricane he is so dishevelled.

A Few have stopped and asked him if he was okay. Some offered him a ride home. Really, he just wanted to be left alone to think. What was he going to tell his mom and dad? There is no way they would believe him, not in a million years?

Upon reaching his house, he stops and looks at it. It seems like his house, nothing has changed. But what about the inside, that is where the smoke dragon came after him. There must be something broken in there. And what about the window to his room? He was sure the smoke dragon was unable to fit through the window, so it is probably all smashed and broken. Of course, he was in the front of the house at the moment so couldn't see that where he stood. But he knew what happened. Boy, is he going to be in trouble. His parents would think he did it, then he would be in for it.

Slowly he comes to the front door. Terrified to go inside, not sure of what he will see. He wonders, are his parents still lying on the dining room table? He takes a deep breath, then says before turning the knob, "Well here goes nothing."

CHAPTER 9
Home

When Max G walked into his house, all was quiet! It still seemed a little dark and gloomy as all the curtains on the windows were closed from the evening before. There didn't seem to be any movement, did this mean that his parents weren't up yet?

He looked a little closer and noticed that nothing seemed to be out of place, not in this room anyway. So he started to walk towards the dining room where he knew his parents had fallen asleep on the table, and the shadow dragon had came after him. He slowly looked around the doorway to see if they were still there.

Nothing, no parents and no mess, everything was back to normal. Did this mean that his parents woke and put everything to rights, or did that just happen with the disappearance of the dragon? This he did not know. His next thought was, where are his parents? If not here, did they go to bed? Well only one way to find out.

Max G slowly ascended the stairs to the bedrooms, he was a little shaky, as this is where he seen the dragon. He just hoped it was gone and wasn't sitting in his mom and dad's room, or his for that matter, waiting for him.

Once he got to the top of the stairs Max G notices that all the doors are closed. He is going to have to open them to see what's inside. For some reason this scares him right out of his wits not knowing what was behind those doors.

He decides to see if his parents are in their room first, so he walks over and takes a deep breath. Then slowly, real slowly he turns the knob. But before he gets it fully open and can see what is in there, a loud snort comes from somewhere inside. This makes Max G jump right out of skin, but then he realizes it is his father snoring. "Whew!" He says with a sigh of relief.

There they were his parents both fast asleep in their bed. Nothing was out of place, considering the night before it had a dragon go through it. Max G shrugs his shoulders and backs out and closes the door behind him. So far things were looking good. Now he had to go to the washroom. He was pretty sure nothing would be in there, so he didn't hesitate this time and just went in. But as he stood relieving himself something behind him started to glow.

He managed to finish going to the bathroom before turning around and seeing the god Morpheus in the bathroom mirror. Max G turns around and is about to start yelling at the god, when he realizes no sound is coming out. For some reason this infuriates him even more.

But the god is trying to settle him down, "be quiet you fool, or my brother will come, and I won't be able to help you!" At this Max G shuts down and just nods.

"Okay, first, congratulations on making it through the night, you have done extremely well. My brother will see this as sign that you are capable. You were able to stay alive without any help! That in itself is saying something. Next, I wanted to give you some advice. You must look around very carefully after you ask for help, as the help was there but you but did not see it. So tonight ask for help but look carefully it will be there. And third, although you think you don't have it in you, you are very brave and are very capable of being the champion my brother needs. Do not doubt yourself. Go with your instincts, you can do it." At this the god looks around and says very quietly, "my brother is coming. He must not know we spoke. Take care." At this he disappears from the mirror and is gone.

Max G couldn't believe what the god told him. "Help was there!" he said. Well Max G didn't see anything. How is it supposed to help if you can't find it? Gods, he was getting very tired of them.

Speaking of tired, Max G just wanted to go lie down and fall asleep, he was so tired, but he knew he had to have a wash. He and his clothes were filthy. So he jumped in the shower which felt like heaven. He wanted more than anything to just stay and have the water wash away all that had happened in the last few hours. But he knew if he wanted to have even an hour or two of sleep, he had to be quick, his mother and father would wake him soon enough.

So he quickly dried off and put on some clean pajamas and laid down on his bed, and went right to sleep. Funny thing was it was the first sleep he had had in forever where he didn't have a nightmare.

CHAPTER 10
The Bribe

Max G woke to his mother calling up the stairs, "Max, your breakfast is ready, time to get up."

The last thing Max wanted to do was get up. His whole body felt so heavy, it was like there were a hundred pillows on top of him, he just felt like he could sleep for days. But he did as he was told. He had never not done what his mother asked of him, he loved her too much. He appreciated all she did for him.

So he got up and put some clean clothes on and brushed his hair. While brushing his hair he looked at himself in the mirror. He looked just awful. He had bags under his eyes and his face had a drooping look to it. "Wow, you look awful Max G." he says out loud to himself. "Wonder what your mother will have to say about that?" Probably nothing, as she will just think he had nightmares all night. Oh well, he thought and took one last look at himself and turned to leave the room.

But just as he turned to leave the room, he thought he heard a voice talking very quietly, like it was mumbling to itself. He stopped in his tracks. He knew that this probably meant that one of the gods was trying to talk to him. He stopped but he wasn't sure if he wanted to talk to them, so he kept walking towards the door, trying to ignore whoever or whatever it was.

He got to the door, but then the something started to talk a little louder so he could hear what they were saying. "Well kid, told you, you would do just fine. You're a champion, and I know you are. I can't wait to see how you kill the nightmare creature. It's like waiting to see what happens at the end of a movie."

Max G turns around and there behind him is the nightmare creature, the god, Phoebetor. He was the creature he had turned into the night before. It would seem he likes this form. But rather than standing straight up like a man, the god has decided to hunch over like an animal. Watching him walk with the donkey hooves in the back and the eagle claws in the front was a little freaky, as the god was pacing back in forth in front of his dresser. Somehow his long straight tail with barbs was swishing back and forth. How he managed not to hit and break anything with it was a mystery to Max G.

Anyway, as soon as he seen this god, something in him turned to fury, he was so mad at this thing he felt like he could kill it with his bare hands. But then he looked at the clawed feet and simmered down. "What in the world made you think that I wanted to do this for the rest of my life and after my life? I am done, I don't ever want to do that again. Do you understand me, find someone else! I don't want to fight your monsters! I want to go back to being me that is it! Got it!" Max yells through gritted teeth, as he did not want his parents to hear him talking to this beast.

Phobetor looks at Max G and says back, "well you know there are perks to befriending the God of Nightmares. I can make sure that all the people you love have all the happiness they deserve in death. I can make sure they don't have to go through the process of being sorted, and make sure they have everything they ever wanted. It will be like...., what do you people call it? Oh yeah, heaven, they will have an eternity of heaven. This I promise you! But you must continue to fight and become my champion. What do you say?"

"What if I decide not to, then what happens to my family?" asks Max G.

"Well, when they die, they will be like everyone else, and will wander the underworld. Sometimes finding goodness, sometimes running into evil. Evil like the nightmares I create, they are eventually sorted to either the good lands or the bad Lands, where they will wonder forever. Either happy or terrified. But like I said if you become my champion, I will make sure they go to the good lands, for sure!" says Phobetor looking a little bored by the fact that he has to bribe this kid to do his bidding.

"Can I think about it? Asks Max G.

Phobetor rolls his dragon eyes and says a little irritated, "do you not realize what I am offering boy, an eternity of happiness to your family." What is there to think about?"

"How do I know you are telling the truth, that you are not lying to me?" asks Max G knowing he was pushing his luck. He knew this god was not going to keep offering him this deal. Because if it was a true deal, it really was a good one. But how was he to know for sure that this was possible?

"You just have to trust me." Says Phobetor. "Going once," and he brings up his eagle claw on his right arm. He is holding the claws up, but one has been bent down. And there are only three claws, so Max G gathered that once he lifted the last, which was the third claw, the deal was up.

"Going twice!" continues Phobetor.

Max G starts to panic, he has no choice, he must take this deal, it would be selfish of him not to. His families eternity of happiness, to his life and afterlife of terror. Max G sees the last claw going down, and he almost screams, "Okay, okay I will do it! But my family's eternal happiness had better be there, when it comes time."

"They will, I give you my word as a god!" says Phobetor. "Well, now that is done ..."

But Max G cuts him off. "What do mean done, don't I have to sign something in blood or sacrificed something in your name?"

Phobetor lets out a little chuckle and says, "Sacrifice? Haven't had a sacrifice in an eternity. Here," he pulls out a piece of parchment in one hand and pen with a gold feather in the other to sign with.

Max G reaches for it and just quickly signs it. He notices that the ink is gold as well.

Phobetor says, "There now you belong to me, and you will train, until I say different. This contract is binding, you will never be able to quit, and you will fight forever. Good luck Champion, I will talk to you soon." Then he disappears.

Max G's mother calls up the stairs again, "Max G breakfast. It is getting cold, come on time to get up.'

"Coming mom, had to get dressed." He calls as he turns to head down the stairs.

CHAPTER 11
The Aunts

At breakfast Max G's mother looked at him with concern. She notices he looks awful but doesn't say anything to him. She knows it is because he has bad nightmares, and he hates when she asks him if he is alright. So she just puts a plate of pancakes and bacon in front of him and says a hearty, "good morning!"

He looks to her with a grateful smile and says, "good morning" back. Then asks both his parents, "Well, what's the plan for this fine Sunday morning?"

"Visit to Aunty May and Aunty Joan's remember?" Says his father reading the paper.

He hadn't remembered and said back, "oh yeah, I forgot. It must have slipped my mind."

Max G's mother comes over and gives his head a rub and says, "That's alright, we know you had a rough start this morning. We will be leaving right after breakfast, as we want to be back at a decent time."

At this Max G starts to panic, "what time are we coming home?" he asks his mother. He knows he has to be back before night falls.

"We were planning on leaving right after supper." Says his father not looking up from the paper he was reading.

Max G knows that it starts getting dark about 9.00, so as long as they don't stay too much longer than right after supper, they should be alright. His aunts live in a small town called Kildore, which is approximately two hours away. He really does not want to be battling a smoke dragon between here and there. So they should be alright, with time to spare.

Although Max G was really hoping to have some time to prepare for the night ahead. I guess I am just going to have to just do my best in the car on the way, he thinks to himself.

Once in the car he has trouble thinking about the night ahead as his mother and father feel it is a fine time to do some family catch up. They want to talk about his life it would seem. About his friends, school and if he had his eye on any girls. Anything and everything Max G did not want to talk about. Finally, after an hour of yapping, Mr. and Mrs. Anderson quiet down and Max G can do some thinking. The only problem is that now it is quiet and with the movement of the car, Max G has been lulled to sleep. And he sleeps for the rest of the trip rather than thinking and planning for the night ahead.

Arriving at the aunt's house was no fun as he woke in a grog and didn't have time to realize it was aunt squishing time. The two of them took turns the minute he got out of the car to pull him into a bear like unescapable hug, you know those ones where you can't breathe for a few minutes, but it feels like hours. And then as soon as you can fill your lungs, it is with the worst smelling flowery perfume you can imagine – I think they call it TOILETTE WATER, or something like that.

Anyway, once that is done, they look at each of us (me and my parents) with this adoring look, like we are the best thing that ever happened to them. And they say things like, "It's been too long, you really need to visit more often!" and "Look how much you have grown since we last seen you. Your mom and dad are going to have to bring you around more often!"

Mom and dad promise to try and come more often, but they do work, and Max has school you know. Mrs. Anderson didn't like using the "G" with Max's name talking to the aunts, only because she didn't want to have to explain things to them. Max told his mom that was alright with him, she could just call him Max in front of the Aunts.

"Thanks buddy!" his mom would say, and smile, "don't worry it will be back to Max G as soon as we are on the ride back home.

CHAPTER 12
The Garden

Lunch wasn't going to be for another hour, so Max asked if he could go over to Tilly's house for a while. Tilly was a friend he had met last time he was at the aunt's house. She was about a year younger than him, but she didn't act like a girl. She liked to rough house with the boys, spit and fart. All the boys around here seemed to like her because she acted so much like a boy. Sometimes it was hard to tell if she was a boy or girl. She had shoulder length dirty blond hair and she always wore a pair of jeans, t-shirt with the word RAD on it, and a jean jacket with dirty white sneakers.

Mrs. Anderson looked down at Max and said, "after lunch, okay? Let's spend a little time with the aunts before rushing off!" This time giving him the, "it's the polite thing to do," look.

"Okay mom, but right after lunch then?"

"Right after lunch will be fine." She answered with a big smile.

So they followed the aunts into the house, where they decided they would go straight through to the backyard where the aunts had a gardener come in and transform it into a beautiful place to sit and enjoy the day. This would be where they would also eat their lunch.

Max decided he really liked the garden as it had paths that you could walk around and benches in odd places so you could just sit and enjoy watching the flowers grow. I know what you are thinking, wow the aunt's house must be huge for them to have a back yard like that.

Well it was, Max's aunts were quite wealthy. They were actually a couple of spinsters who had no children of their own. But the two of them were always so close when growing up, that they decided to go into business together. They owned a real estate business that flourished, and they made millions.

Anyway, back to their house. You know those old Victorian mansions. Well, their house was double the size of those, and the yards were extremely big as well. The aunt's had servants that did all their cooking, cleaning, and gardening. They didn't have to do anything. Which was good because they were really getting up there. Aunt May was the younger of the two at 79, while Aunt Joan was 81. Both walked with canes but still kept their posture. They weren't like most old people who after a while found themselves bent over like the hunchback of Notre Dame. No, they both sat up straight and proper.

Anyway Max found himself wondering through the paths of the huge garden, there were statues made of stone as well as bushes that were cut into shapes like frogs and lizards. Max thought whoever the gardener was he sure had some talent.

He was wandering and looking at all the wonderful things when he came to a beautiful fountain. There were two nymphs that stood in the middle that poured water out of each of their buckets and into the fountain below. Max thought this fountain had to be probably the most beautiful thing he had ever seen. As he got closer, he looked into the water, and there swimming in the depths were many goldfish. Not those tiny fish you get for your little fishbowl, but humongous ones. Ones that were as long as his forearm, if not longer. There were so many, he didn't know how they could find room to swim.

He sat on the edge of the fountain for a while and just kind of got lost in watching the water flow and the fish swimming, when out of nowhere something shiny had caught his eye. It shone from the depths of the fountain. He just thought it was probably a coin someone threw in to make a wish. But the shiny thing seemed to follow him. He tried to get away from it so it wouldn't shine right in his eyes, but it didn't seem to want to let up, it would follow him whichever way he turned.

So he decided he would reach in and see what it was that was causing such a sparkle. When he got to the bottom, which felt extremely weird because the fish were bumping into his arm, he felt something long and straight, so he pulled it out. In his hands was a dagger. The dagger was in the shape of a dragon, and it had eyes made of rubies. The knife itself was beautiful, it shone like someone had taken great care of it.

Then out of nowhere a voice sounded. He started and tried to hide the dagger. Max really didn't want anybody to know, or they would take it from him. But looking around he couldn't see anyone. So he relaxed thinking it was his imagination.

Then the voice sounded again, this time it sounded like it was coming from the fountain. So Max had a look into the depts, sure enough there was Morpheus, the God of Dreams. His face was all distorted because all the fish were swimming through it, but it was definitely him.

"What do you want?" Max asks rather rudely.

"I want to help; just thought I would show you how to ask for things. But if you don't want my help, I will leave." Says the God of Dreams, looking like his feelings are hurt.

"No its okay, please come back, I am sorry I was rude. I know you are just trying to help. I guess I just wasn't expecting you that is all." Says Max in a sorry tone.

"Well how do you like it?" asks Morpheus. "The dagger I mean?"

"You gave me this, I don't know how to thank you, it is absolutely beautiful. Thank you! But why did you give me this?" Max asks.

"I wanted to show you that you still have control. That you can still ask for things. You just have to find them in the proper place." Explains Morpheus.

"Mirrors and water are a kind of way to get into the dream world, if there is any water or a mirror around. This is your weapon, I will be able to get anything you need through them, just ask. Oh! Oh! My brother is coming, he must not know we spoke. Take care Dream Champion, tonight is the night you will rid your world of the monster, I am sure of it!" Morpheus says all this in a kind of whisper than disappears.

It is at this time Max can hear his mother calling him for lunch, so he says a soft "thank you" into the fountain, then heads back to where he came.

CHAPTER 13
Tilly

It was after lunch, and Max wanted go find Tilly. The only problem it was only after his lunch. The aunts and his parents were still eating their cucumber sandwiches and cream of broccoli soup. "Yuck!" Thought max. He was glad the aunts didn't expect him to eat that grossness. He got to have bologna with mustard sandwich and chicken noodle soup, which is his all-time favorite. The aunts were good that way, always making sure Max got whatever he wanted. They loved him so much. He loved them as well; he just didn't like hanging out and talking about warts and arthritis and such. He liked to be out playing and exploring with his friends.

Aunt Joan looked over at Max and could see he was done his lunch and was now just sitting there to be polite, so she let him off the hook and said, "Why my boy, you should go exploring, no sense in sitting here and hearing about us old folks. You go and run and find some friends. I believe that Tilly girl is still around, my sister and I see her and her friends sometimes when we leave the grounds. They play at the park most often."

Max is so totally grateful to Aunt Joan and stands up and says, "Thanks Aunt Joan. I think I will go and see if I can find her," and he looks to his mom to see if it was alright. She gives him a big smile and a nod but tells him to be back by 5.00 o clock for supper.

He waves back at her just to let her know he heard, for he is already close to the front corridor. Once out the front corridor he must run down the drive and through some pretty high gates that get closed every night. If you were to stop at the gate and look back at the house you would think it was one of the most beautiful houses you ever seen, but at night it had to be the creepiest. A few times Max came back too late and found out just how creepy. But not this time, he was not going to hold his family up, he needed to get back home. He was not fighting the dragon here and that was that.

When he got out of the gate there was a sidewalk that turned to the left, which took you to the end of his aunt's property, so it was quite a way. There was a gate all a long it with vines all through it so you couldn't see onto his aunt's property. But once he did get to the end of the block, he crossed the street and went down one more block. He passed other houses, not houses like his aunts, just ordinary houses for ordinary people. They were at least 6 on each side of the street, with trees planted out front, and driveways to get into each. It was in one of these houses that Tilly lived, but he couldn't remember which one. So he went to the end of this block and crossed another street, for on the corner was the park that Tilly and her friends like to hang out.

When he got there, he didn't see anyone except a mother and her 2-year-old playing on one of the little slides. But the park was quite large, and had many structures, Tilly could be hiding at any one of them.

The first one he looked in was the one at the top of the structure, it was like a little playhouse with windows and such. No one there. But he stopped and listened, and he could swear he could hear a couple of kids talking, almost in a whisper. So he went down the slide and went into the plastic structure underneath the rest, it too was set up like a little house, it had windows and a door as well.

When he poked his head in there low and behold was his friend Tilly and someone else, he did not expect, it was another girl. When Tilly seen him, she shouted at him, "No boys allowed, get out!" This shocked the heck out of Max, but he was persistent.

"Tilly really, why can't a boy come in, especially one who came all this way to see his friend he hasn't seen since last summer?" Max asks in a kind of hurt tone.

It was then it would seem that Tilly realized who it was, got up and came outside the structure and gave him a big hug and said "sorry, but Nellie and I are a little mad at the boys around here at the moment."

"Oh how come?" asks Max.

"It's a kind of a long story," she says kind of dismissing the question. "Hey Nellie come meet my friend from Minnedosa. He's not liked those other boys; he won't push you or call you silly names." Then Tilly kind of talks under her breath, "it's like the boys around here have gone crazy or something."

Max was just going to get her to repeat what she said, as he couldn't quite hear her, when her friend Nellie stepped out of the little playhouse. Max almost forgot to swallow. He had never seen such a pretty girl in his life. In Max's eyes Nellie was the perfect girl, she had long black hair, past her bum, perfect teeth, and skin so smooth. She was actually quite tall, just a couple of inches shorter than him. She also had the greenest eyes; they were like emeralds. When she came out of the structure and walked over to him to shake his hand, it would seem, she had the most beautiful smile, with the most beautiful cheek bones, as well. He also notices a little tear that's sitting just below her eye. It made her look vulnerable, and he wanted to fight to the death anyone who had made her cry.

Shake hands! All this girl wanted to do was shake hands! When all he wanted to do was take her in his arms and kiss her. But it would seem he was having a hard time just not staring at her like she was some kind alien. He gave his head a shake and came forward to shake her hand, but when he went to talk and say, "Nice to meet you" it came out "ummm, ummm." He found his brain went on holiday and he couldn't say what he wanted.

But then Tilly seeing all this rolls her eyes and says, "Oh great, not you too! What is wrong with boys, they get around Nellie and they act so silly, well you better not be nasty to her, or you will have me to deal with." She scorns Max as she gives him a little punch in the arm.

This little punch wakes Max out of his, well; whatever it is that has come over him, and he says to Nellie, "I'm sorry, it is very nice to meet you." Then he turns to Tilly, "I promise I won't be nasty, and if I see anyone else being nasty, I will help you fight them." Then he looks at Nellie and says, "I don't know why anyone would be nasty to you but let them try when I am there. I'm not very strong but I don't like people picking on my friends."

Nellie looked at Max then and said, "Thank you Max, I really appreciate that."

Tilly looks at both of them and thinks they are both off their rockers, not realizing that her friend Nellie likes Max like Max likes Nellie. They are both looking at each other like there is no one else there, so Tilly comes over and waves her hand in between their faces, and says, "hello, I'm here as well you know."

Nellie and Max stop staring at each other, and Max says to Tilly, "We know that!" then steps away from Nellie feeling a little embarrassed.

Nellie too does the same, she can't figure out why she likes this boy but she really does.

That afternoon, the three of them spend time walking around the town and getting some junk food from the local grocery store and well, just hanging out and telling each other about themselves. Mostly Nellie wanted to hear about Max and Max wanted to hear about Nellie. Poor Tilly was starting to feel like a third wheel, but stuck it out anyway, as Max was her friend not Nellie's.

They had a great time catching up, but 5.00 o clock came fast, and it was time for Max to head back to his aunts for supper. He really did not want to go, he wanted to spend all his time with Nellie. So he asked the girls for their phone numbers so he could call them, and vice versa. He gave them his phone number. He said he would call soon and ran off to his aunts with many waves. "Goodbye." He yells back wishing he didn't have to leave.

CHAPTER 14
"Oh No!"

When Max got closer to his aunt's house, he could tell something wasn't right. He could see a red and blue light flashing above the fence that surrounded the grounds, this made him run.

As he got closer to the gate to get into the grounds, he could tell something definitely wasn't right. When he turned into the grounds, he could see an ambulance sitting in front of the house. It had backed up to the house with its two back doors wide open, looking like it was waiting for a victim.

Max didn't know what to think, what had happened? He ran even faster. He hoped no one was hurt badly. What if it was his mother or father? Again, this thought made him run quicker.

Finally he got to the front door, and just as he got there two ambulance people were bringing someone out on a stretcher, it was his Aunt May. She did not look too good. She had a mask over her face, and she looked like death had already dealt its blow. But then she blinked, and Max knew she wasn't dead.

His mother was with her, talking to her, telling her everything was going to be alright. Max's dad also came out the front door helping Aunt Joan outside. He looked at Max like he was grateful that he was there and said, "Max it looks like we will be staying longer. Your mother and I are going to take Aunt Joan to the hospital so she can be with Aunt May, they think she might have had a stroke. You can stay or come, it's up to you." As he was saying this, he was helping Aunty Joan into the car.

All Max could think of was, now what am I going to do? His father took the look as one of shock, and when he got Aunty Joan in the car. He came over to Max and put his arm around him and said "I know this is all so much to bring in, but I am sure your Aunty May will be alright. Maybe you should come with us, this house is a bit scary when no one is home except the help. Especially at night."

Max turns and looks at his father and says, "No, it's okay I will be alright here. You go to be with mom and Aunt Joan." All the time trying to think where the best place would be to fight the smoke dragon. Not that Max didn't care about his aunt, but he knew now that he would have to fight this scary dragon on unfamiliar territory, and he was terrified.

It was this terrified look that made his father hug him in tight and promise him everything was going to be alright. "We will be spending the night so you know where you will be sleeping if we are not back by bedtime. If you are hungry the cooks have made supper. Go and enjoy! We will be back soon, no worries!" He tries to give Max a reassuring smile then turns and gets in the car with Aunt Joan, who also looks worried.

They both give a last wave and head out of the drive, then through the gate and are gone, leaving Max standing there feeling what? Max wonders if he feels alone, scared, hungry, and confused by everything that just happened. He just stood and stared at the gate everyone had passed through, he didn't want to move for some reason. It was like he was stuck.

Then just like that his brain pictures Nellie, and everything seems to come to the surface. First, he needs to eat, he is starving, and then he needs to make a plan of some kind. Where is the best place to kill the beast?

He turns and runs into the house and goes to the kitchen, there are the cooks putting away the supper they had prepared for everyone.

But then they see Max and smile, they are more than willing to get him his supper. One of the lady cooks gets him to sit at a table in the kitchen while they make him a plate of roast beef, mashed potatoes, mixed veggies and a bun. She also brings a glass of milk and big piece of chocolate cake. She brings it all on a tray so he can take it and eat it wherever he wants to. Max thanks them all very much and leaves the kitchen with his tray.

He thought about going into the living room and watching TV while he ate but then he thought, no I better spend some time thinking about where I need to fight this dragon. He decides to go to his room. There in his room is a big old desk that has a big mirror behind. He thinks – Oh great! This is probably where the smoke dragon will come through if I am still here. Or maybe just maybe the god of dreams – Morpheus will want to talk, well maybe he can give some advice.

He sits his tray down and starts eating, waiting to see if the God of Dreams will show up. He doesn't want to call as his brother the God of Nightmares, Phobetor; might hear him calling and get mad. Then Morpheus wouldn't be able to help Max when he really needed the help. So he sat and ate his supper, waiting to see if the God would show up. But he didn't, his brother must be around.

Oh well, he finishes his supper and takes his tray to the kitchen, where he asks one of the cooks, "don't suppose there is a lake or river around here is there?" The cook looks at him kind of funny, but then smiles and says, "Why yes, of course; we have both of those. You have to travel to the North of the town and there is a lake, and also a river runs through the outskirts. There is a bridge that people have to cross in order to get into town there."

"How long would it take someone to walk to the bridge from here?" asks Max.

The cook gives him another suspicious look and says, "You are not planning on going there now, are you? It is getting late and your parents would probably want you to stay here."

Max says, "No I am just bored and wondered is all."

"Well to wonder is okay, it would probably take someone to walk there probably 20 minutes to half an hour. Not long at all." Answers the lady cook.

Max spins around and at the same time says, "Thank you very much!" then he runs off leaving the cook to wonder if she did the right thing.

Well so far that is good, there is water. The last time the water saved his life. That was the most important part. Now to think up a weapon that would kill a smoke dragon. He thinks a blooming tornado would do the job, but Max didn't think he could get that as a weapon. So he tries to go over some of the weapons he has conjured up in his dreams. They all seem hopeless, as fighting a monster in the real world is a great deal different then in his dreams. The danger seems a bit more permanent.

In the end he decides on fire proof robes, ones that are easy to just throw on, and something like a magical sword that will go through the shadow part of the dragon, one that will penetrate a hole to its heart.

The problem is, is that Max doesn't know if he can call up magical items or just ordinary items. But he is going to try and find out, because ordinary items are not going to do the trick.

He has now decided on his weapon and place of choice, it was now time to go and find the place of choice. On his way out he sees a watering can the gardeners use to water the flowers; he grabs this for extra back-up and is on his way. The sun seems to be going down rather quickly!

CHAPTER 15
"The Fight"

Rather than going straight down the streets that go to the park, Max turns to go north this time, which also runs along his aunt's property. Once he hits the end of his aunt's property, he keeps going at least another 5 blocks before he comes to the edge of town. From there he turns right as he can see the bridge that the cook was talking about from there.

He walks another two blocks and finally comes to the bridge, where the river is flowing quite strong. This is good, just in case Max needs a fast get away. But he must get to the lake, that is where he will be making his stand. That is where he is hoping to be able to call upon the God Morpheus for help. See, as long as there is a mirror effect he should be able to call to the other side, the dream side for help. According to the God Morpheus anyway. Max is only hoping that it is true.

He crosses the bridge, once across he heads east to get to the lake. There he sees there is a sandy little beach that isn't too far from the rivers opening. He walks up to the lake, and by this time it has become quite dark. It is at that point where the sun has just gone down, but there is still a little light. He walks up to the lake and looks down into the depths, and almost jumps out of his skin.

There in the depths is his Aunt May, and behind her is a glowing man smiling down at her. What is going on? Max wants to know but is too shocked to say this out loud. Why is his aunt with the God of Nightmares?

Finally, his Aunt May looks at Max and says, "Thank you Max, I knew you were special from the moment I laid eyes on you. This is the best gift you could bring an old woman." As she is saying this, she seems to be getting younger as she talks. She looks so happy; Max just looks down at her and tries not to cry but can't help it. He really did love his aunt and he was going to miss her.

Then her and the god of nightmares turn and walk into the light that radiates behind them. The smile on his aunt's face letting Max know she was going to a happy place, and that made all this madness worth it. He would fight whatever monsters were sent his way, no matter what. But this thought was erased from his mind, for just like that as their reflection disappeared the reflection of a heavy breathing smoke dragon took their place, and Max almost swallowed his tongue.

He was too shocked to move, he knew the dragon wasn't in the water, it was hovering right behind him. The fact that it hadn't snapped him up in its mouth full of sharp teeth yet was kind of strange. It had Max right where it needed him. But it was this hesitation that gave Max the time to shout out what he wanted from the watery depths, then Max dove deep into the water.

I don't think the dragon expected that and kind of went to go forward and follow, but realized as a smoke dragon it would not be a good idea to go into the water. So he waited, he knew that the kid couldn't stay down there forever. But he got bored and started blowing fire back and forth along the water, maybe he would be able to see where the kid was in the water at least.

Sure enough the boy ascended from the water, but it was a little way off from where the dragon was. When he came out of the water he was no longer Max the boy, but Max the great Dragon Hunter. He was robed in fire resistant material, and he a magic sword that glowed red. This meant that it was able to penetrate the smoke and be able to get to the dragon's heart.

The dragon could feel the change in the boy, he was no longer a frightened little kid, but a man who was sure he was going to get his prey. This made the dragon a little leery, but the dragon knew he had to destroy this boy no matter what. He sent a great big flame towards the boy. The boy did not run but stood there with his sword in front of him, which held the flames at bay. The dragon expected Max to be ash when it was done blowing its fire but was shocked to see that his flames did nothing. Again, the dragon wondered why.

But it was at this time another creature came from the other end of the beach, it seemed to be chasing someone. Both Dragon and boy looked over. There, coming toward them was a dinosaur almost like a t-rex, but this creature had a face like a bird. It had a beak instead of mouth full of teeth, and on its back, it had two wings that looked like they came from a baby bird, they were little leathery looking things. They had no feathers and were shaped like a baby bird. Also, it had this thing on the top of its head which made it look like a rooster. It was red all over but had orange eyes. The rest of it could have been a t-rex, as it was just as big and had the little arms out front and everything.

When Max looked closer, he could see the person it was chasing, and low and be hold it was Nellie. Why would one of his creatures chase her down?

But then out of nowhere she stopped and said some words over and over again, and as she told them something came flying out of the water and kept hitting the dinosaur bird over and over again. It looked as if it wasn't doing much damage, but then the creature stopped, and noticed Max and the smoke dragon. The next thing Max knows is that the creature is now coming toward him and ignoring Nellie. This is great, thinks Max, now Nellie can get way.

But it is not Max the creature wants, but the smoke dragon, and the smoke dragon wants this creature. The two dream creatures smash into one another and fight like there is no tomorrow. Max is trying not to get trampled in the process.

Meanwhile Nellie doesn't turn and run away, she decides she is going to dodge getting trampled and runs over to where Max is standing. "Hey you there, who are you and why have you brought this creature to my territory?"

Max is again dumbfounded by her; his tongue gets all tied up and he can't talk. All he can do is look at her, she so beautiful. She has her hair tied back in a ponytail and she is wearing camouflage jeans and a black muscle shirt. She looks just like a girl commando. She has such a tough look to her right now, like nothing, nowhere could beat her in a fight. Wow! Max thinks. She is so amazing!

As she got closer, Max decided to pull his hood down so she can see who it is, and she stops short. Meanwhile, the two creatures are still fighting each other tooth and nail, and they don't look as if they were planning on letting up.

Nellie gets over her shock and comes over and grabs Max by the arm, none too gently, and pulls him so they are getting away from the battle. She doesn't let go until she feels they are far enough away that they won't get trampled. Then she pushes Max down, so he sits down on a grassy knoll she has decided they are going to sit at.

Then she sits beside him and says with a mad look to her, "Explain!"

So Max tells Nellie everything. It felt good to be able to tell someone. He thought he was alone in this path that was set out for him.

Nellie listens then tells him that he is not alone obviously, but that two champions are not usually this close together as all it does is make their creatures fight one another until they kill each other.

Then that means the champion has to try and do it all over again the next night. They do not get the credit for the kill.

Max says, "I am sorry this is only my second night, and I don't know all the rules yet, in fact I know none of the rules. But either way it couldn't have been helped, not with his aunt going into the hospital."

This Nellie agreed and told him that, "It was alright, she would just have to do it again tomorrow." But then asks, "You not here another night, are you?"

"I really don't know what my parents will want to do, as I am pretty sure my aunt died last night." Then he tells her about seeing his aunt in the lake.

Nellie answers with, "Yes that is our reward, to see our family members going to a happy place when they die. It is the best reward ever!'

Max has to agree, seeing his aunt as happy as she was made him feel extremely good inside.

"Well now what do we do? Do we wait until the creatures kill each other?" asks Max?

She now looks at him with a different kind of look and says, "Yes, we must stay, but we might as well stay busy, and she leans over to him and gives him a big kiss.

CHAPTER 16
Angel

Max was so, so... he didn't know what it was he felt. Elation? In love? All he knew was that he was just so happy, he was sure this was what cloud 9 felt like.

That morning when he came into the house, he could see his parents on the couch holding each other. His mother with a tissue to her nose. They looked like they could be awake, but they were not, they were asleep. The dream sleep that happened when the dragon came to fight. They would wake not even noticing the way they fell asleep.

Max didn't think he would be able to sleep, all he could think about was Nellie and her soft lips touching his. They spent most of the rest of the evening kissing and doing very little talking. For an 11-year-old boy, this was a dream come true and he never wanted it to end. He wanted to stay at his aunt's house forever and never leave.

Well he knew that was never going to happen, so he just made a plan to phone and let Nellie know when they were leaving so maybe she could come and say "good bye."

He went upstairs and started to undress and put his pajamas on, when again out of the blue the God Phobetor would show himself. "Well, boy it seems you have met Nellie, she is one of my best champions. She probably already told you what happens when two monsters fight instead of the champions? The champions do not get credit for the kill."

"Yes, she might have mentioned it." Max says with a grin on his face. He still can't stop thinking of Nellie, even with the God of Nightmares talking to him.

"Alright, as long as you know, that way you will do your best to avoid it next time. I will not have a battle between monsters every night. That is not how things work. Understood?" Asks Phoebetor?

"Yes, it is understood," Max says even though he's really not listening to what the God is saying to him.

"Good then, get some sleep, you will do battle again tonight." Then the God of Nightmares disappeared.

Max says out loud to himself, "Good night," to whom he didn't know, but then he rolled over and went to sleep. He dreamed of a girl. She was the most beautiful girl ever. In fact, she was so beautiful the gods turned her into a goddess or an angel if you like, so she could be beautiful forever. There was a light that shone from her, and she smiled down at Max and looked into his eyes. What he saw was beauty in eternity, it went on forever.

The next thing Max knows is his mother is sitting beside him on his bed nudging him awake. She looks so sad, Max thought, nothing like the angel he seen in his dreams. Course, he thought his mother was beautiful, but nothing compared to the beauty in his dreams. She brought complete and utter happiness with her, wherever she went.

Max's mother looked down at him and said, "Wake up sleepy head, its 11.00 o clock. Breakfast is over and the cooks are starting on lunch. Your father and I have some bad news to tell you, so please get up and get dressed."

"It's okay mom, I know about Aunt May, she died last night, didn't she?" asks Max.

"Well yes, but how did you know?" She asks curious.

Max tells his mother in the most consoling way he can. "I had a dream about her mom, I had a dream about Aunt May and mom she was young again and so very beautiful. She came to me as an angel, and she is happy where she is. She told me so, she told me not to be sad, and I was to tell the rest of the family as well."

Max's mom looked at Max like she didn't know what to think. Did he really dream this or did he just make it up to make her feel better. But by the look on his face, he didn't seem to be lying. So she said, "Max that is beautiful. I hope you are right, and she really is happy, knowing that makes things so much more bearable. Either way please get up and get dressed. Aunty Joan is taking it very hard; she and Aunt May were extremely close you know."

"Okay mom I won't be long." He says as she moves so he can jump out of bed and get dressed.

She leaves him to get dressed and Max runs around the room picking up his clothes where he left them. With everything that was going on he never even gave a thought to poor Aunt Joan. She must be devastated.

He hurried as fast as he could and ran down the stairs. He stopped in the living room, and no one was there, so he headed towards the back of the house where the garden was. There they all were, his mom and dad and Aunt Joan. They all looked so sad, like it was the end of the world.

When they all seen Max come in, they all tried to put on a better face. But Max knew what was going on, and decided he needed to tell everyone about his dream.

When Aunt Joan heard she seemed to feel a little better, but still life without her sister beside her was still too much for her to bear. "There is nothing left for me." She said out loud, then went quiet and never said another word. And she didn't until the day she died 2 months later.

Max felt bad for her, but he knew she was right, and he also knew that in death she would be happy. He would miss both the aunts, even though they were a little senile, but they were both generous and loved open heartedly.

The last thing talked about at the lunch table that day was that it was their plan to stay with Aunt Joan until the funeral, which would be 3 days from then. Then they would need to make arrangements for someone to come and look after Aunt Joan. They could not leave her there alone.

All Max heard out of the conversation was they were staying, and that meant he could spend more time with Nellie. Not that he didn't care about his aunt, but right now it just seemed as if Nellie was the one thing on his brain, and he just couldn't concentrate on anything else.

So after lunch he told his mom and dad he would be at the park with Tilly, as he wasn't ready to tell them about Nellie just yet. They would only ask questions as they always did.

"Of course," was their answer, go! You don't have to hang out here, go and have fun!"

CHAPTER 17
Nellie

Hanging out with Nellie was possibly the best time Max could remember in his lifetime. He really liked Nellie, and all he wanted to do was spend time kissing her.

All she wanted to do was talk about dream champion stuff. She wanted to train him so he wouldn't have trouble with his monsters. Nellie wanted him to learn how to dodge the monsters, not just run away. She also wanted him to know, what were the best kind of weapons to ask for when killing his monsters? Where were the best places to be when his monsters showed up? After all, the smoke dragon wasn't going to be the only monster he fought, now that he was a Dream Champion.

These were all things Nellie wanted to teach him, if only he would listen. She too liked the kissing part, but one day Tilly had come around the corner and seen them sitting on a slide, kissing each other. She turned really red and spun around and they never seen her again that day.

At the time the two of them thought, well; be mad then, you'd think she would be happy for us instead. It was a selfish thought and they both felt extremely bad about it later on, and only wanted to make it up to her. But she avoided them and wouldn't come out when they called on her at her house, and she wouldn't answer her phone.

It wasn't until Max left that Tilly came out and played with Nellie again. It would seem she was mad at Max because he was taking advantage of her friend, and no matter what Nellie told her Tilly stayed mad at Max. Which in Nellie's mind meant that Tilly was jealous. So instead of being mad at Tilly for hating Max she just talked about how wonderful Max was and how glad she was that Tilly had introduced them. Eventually Tilly just started to feel good about the relationship rather than bitter. As she seen how happy Nellie was and she liked to take credit for her happiness.

Anyway back to the two champions, Nellie spent a great deal of time with Max showing him how to tuck and roll, and used a stick to jab and practice throwing at a target.

She talked about the different kinds of creatures she had fought since she started, and what kind of weapons she used to fight them.

The second night when the creatures came, they again let them fight each other, and again they got in trouble from Mr. God – Phobetor. He did not like the fact that the children were using this as time to spend together, he wanted them fighting their monsters.

They told the god, "No worries they were going to fight them on the third night. That they were planning on splitting up far enough that they would not see each other." Thus, he was satisfied and said, "So be it!"

The third day, as much as they didn't want to, they both followed the river in opposite directions, they had to go quite far from each other so they started right after the evening meal, with Max's mom reminding him to get home early as they would be going home in the morning. Of course, this was not going to happen, Max wouldn't get home until he had killed his dragon and who knew how long that would take.

He travelled down the river for hours, at least 3, when he came to spot that looked like it was fairly deserted of people and houses, and there was a sandy shoreline that had still puddles where he could ask for his weapons he would need.

It was approximately 10 o'clock and the dragon would be here any moment, and he would find out just how much he learned through Nellie's training.

He learned not to be sitting when he thought the monster was going to show, as usually you had to dodge whatever it was going to do to you right away. But he also learned that as long as there is still water or a mirror handy you can call for whatever you need from quite a way away. She never had any trouble calling weapons from a mile away. So, he stood over the puddle, but as soon as he heard the monsters breathing, he screamed what he wanted right way from the puddle. He wanted a magic sword that would rip through a smoke dragons hide, and armor and shield that would help keep him safe from the fire the dragon breathed. All these things magically showed up on him, one minute he was just wearing jeans and a t-shirt the next he is wearing armor and carrying a sword and shield. The shield with a picture of a smoke dragon on it.

As soon as he had this on, which took mere seconds and was happening while Max was moving, for as he screamed out what he needed he rolled and dodged the monsters' claws and fire at the same time. All the time the outfit was placing itself on him. Once dressed for battle he found he had confidence. He was not the scared kid that was running away from this beast a few days ago. He was a hunter now, and he was going to kill this dragon. Whatever it took!

CHAPTER 18
Dragon Down

You would think that once you were totally ready to fight a fire breathing smoke dragon that it would be easy to do. Unfortunately, doesn't matter how ready or how confident you are, it's not the easiest thing to do.

Max is finding that he is spending way too much time dodging and running from the dragon's flames and claws and can't seem to find a way to get to the dragon's heart. And because he is spending so much time dodging and running, he is getting extremely tired. He needs to find a way to get the upper hand, but he can't think. The dragon has him constantly on the move.

If only he could fly or leap, that might help him to get the advantage, but unfortunately, he did not have wings. But then he found that the next leap he made he went quite far, farther than he thought he could jump in his lifetime. But as he jumped, he could see himself in the still puddle that gave him his armor and found that when he leaped over the puddle there was a picture of a boy in full armor, with a shield and magic sword, but could see that the boy did have wings. Big, beautiful wings, wings that you would see on an angel.

Max could hardly believe it! When he landed, he didn't find that he had to dodge the dragon this time. He was far enough away that he could take a moment and take it all in. He was not sure, but he thought, how can I use them? I have never had wings before. But then the dragon came, and Max turned and jumped, rather than rolling away, and found himself in the air, flying!

He could fly! All he had to do was think that he was flying, and this made him fly, it was just like thinking about moving an arm or leg. That's how easy it was! Now! Thought Max, that dragon is in for it!

The dragon could sense the change in Max. He sensed something different the minute he showed himself. This boy wasn't scared of him anymore, but the dragon was so confident in his abilities that he thought, there is no way this boy will kill me. I'm a ferocious dragon, no one can kill me. But he was getting tired of playing with his prey, it was now time to kill the boy. He had fun these past nights, but he wanted to move on. So now the boy was going to die.

Max could sense the change in the dragon. He sensed that the dragon was now trying so very hard to kill him that it was going to be either him or the dragon that lived. So he circled the dragon up in the air. He found that with his new wings that he was faster than the dragon. All he had to do was think of where he wanted to go and was there in a split second.

Once Max figured out how to be faster than the dragon, for a dragon is large and clumsy, while Max could move with a thought. Max knew exactly what he had to do. He must fly straight up in the air and spin right back around and dive at the dragon. Dive with the magic sword ready to strike. This Max did, hitting the dragon with such fierceness and strength, the dragon didn't know what hit him, until the sword was deep in its chest, where it pierced its heart!

Once the sword penetrated the dragon's heart, the heart seemed to crumble. Once it started, the rest of the dragon crumbled as well. But not without a last roar that probably could have been heard back in town. Then all that was left, was a few wisps of smoke, then they too disappeared, and that was the last of the smoke dragon.

Max couldn't believe what he had done. He had killed a ferocious fire breathing, smoke dragon, right here on earth. Not in his dreams but here among people. Well, technically he was in a field. But he was still earth bound, and he did it with a magic sword and wings! He had wings that was the best part of the battle, he loved this part. It was not something he thought he could ask for, but there they were! And they had saved his life.

As Max was thinking, all his stuff, armor, sword, and wings all disappeared. It didn't matter, he knew if he needed them they would be there. Max walked up to the still puddle and looked down into it and said, "Thanks buddy, you saved my life." Then out of nowhere a glow came from the puddle, and out popped the one god he didn't want to see at that moment. The God of Nightmares himself, Phobetor.

He was a glowing man this time instead of the ugly creature he usually chose, which Max was happy about.

"Well, my boy you did it, and I am never so proud, and as I told you before I will make sure your family members will always be happy when they have moved on." Says Phobetor.

"But now something has happened that has never happened before, and I am going to need the help of all my champions in the real world. It seems gateways from the underworld are opening up all over the world and my creations are getting out. Those champions that are in the underworld cannot follow them to kill them, they would just turn to dust in this world."

Phobetor continues, "The other problem is that you won't be able to kill the creatures here as they were born in the underworld that is where they will need to die. So, you can put them to sleep if you like, but it will be very hard to lure them back to the gateway. This is what must be done with every one of the creatures. They must be lured not killed and sent back to where they came from. Is that understood, I will leave you to explain to your girlfriend. You will know when one is close, as the world will fall into a deep slumber when one gets close."

Max is shocked, how could this have happened? He has a million questions, but finds he wants to know about the gateways, and asks, "How in the heck are gateways opening up? What could open them, also why can't you close them? Is there a way we can close them? For what's the use of getting the creatures to a gateway if it won't close behind them?"

"All good questions," says Phobetor, "which is why I am giving you this." He hands over a rod with glowing blue light at the end. "This will help you to find the gateway, when it turns red you are very close. Once you get the monster inside plunge this sceptre into the gateway and it will close the gateway forever."

"Now if you don't mind, I must go. I must go to the other champions and give them a sceptre and instructions on how to use it. Goodbye Max G you really did a very good job on that dragon, keep up the good work!" Then just like that he was gone, and the world became dark once more. Dark except the glow of the sceptre.

Max looked at the sceptre and thought, how am I going to hide you. But at the thought the sceptre turned itself into a flashlight. Max just laughed and spoke out loud to himself, "Wow they just think of everything don't they." Then he turned to go back toward Kildore where he hoped to meet up with Nellie before going home. Hopefully, she is waiting for him.

CHAPTER 19
Other Champions

Sure enough Nellie had been waiting for Max, as Phobetor gave her a sceptre as well, but told her to wait for Max who would give her instructions and the low down on what was happening.

Both wondered if this meant they were expected to travel the world. They were only kids; it was one thing to fight on a nightly bases. They never went too far from home. But to actually travel, they didn't have the means, not without their parents getting worried about them. It wasn't like they could tell their parents and expect them to give rides every night or money for buses.

No there was no way, but Phobetor did mention other champions, they will have to look after those other places, but how could Max and Nellie know it was getting done? Internet! Maybe they could start a web page and see if they could get other champions to talk. It was worth a try.

That night Max said his goodbyes to Nellie and Tilly, telling them both that he would keep in touch. For he was leaving in the morning to go back to Minnedosa, and they would probably not see each other until next summer. But they all promised to keep in touch. They would write and phone, and together Max and Nellie would make a web page that other champions could talk to them through, and vice versa.

The web page said, "To All Dream Champions of the World," and found that they received more than 50 hits the first week. They were definitely not alone. They met so many more and found that each had so many ideas on how to lure the monsters into the gateways. It was also easy to find out where the monsters were popping out as this too got told to everyone.

"It really does work just like Phobetor says, the sceptre; it glows a real deep red when you get close to a gateway," says one of the champions on their new webpage.

A girl named Emily from California had a three headed cobra, that when it stood up it was as tall as their house.

In Japan a sister and brother champion group, which Max and Nellie thought was not possible. But guessed it was because they were twins that they were grouped together. Had some kind of hairy beast like a Bigfoot, but it too was so big that it was as tall as their water tower.

There were so many different kinds of creatures all over the world. It was a good thing that there were so many champions out there. Especially with Phobetor recruiting every single day. This was good because there was no way Max and Nellie would have been able to fight all the monsters on their own.

After a while Max and Nellie found they had so many creatures of their own to fight right there in Minnedosa and Kildore. That they were in constant training, which taught them they were able to fight and lure the creatures, then send them back easier and easier every time they did it. But for some reason even with the special sceptres Phobetor gave them the doors still weren't closing behind them. Something or someone was keeping them open. Somehow the champions would have to find out what or who it was. Phobetor insists it was not him, and that he is just as mad as they are.

The only good part is that the champions on the dream side are waiting to kill the creatures as soon as they enter the underworld. So the same creatures at least aren't coming back. But new ones are always slipping through, which is keeping all the dream champions, both on earth and in the underworld extremely busy.

They must find a way to close the gateways forever, but how? They must find the answer, and soon! But that is for another champion to find out. So we will say good bye to Max and Nellie and wish them luck, as every champion needs a great deal. Good Luck!

www.ingramcontent.com/pod-product-compliance
Lightning Source LLC
Chambersburg PA
CBHW031420131125
35288CB00038B/542